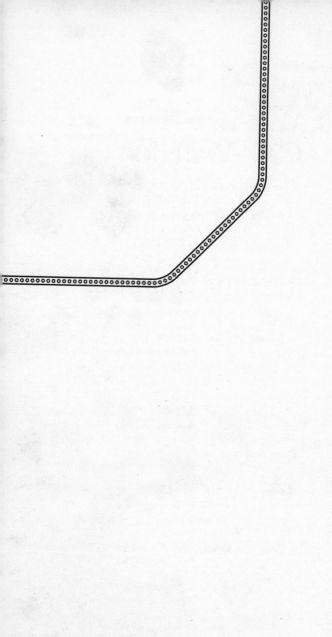

Waterloo–City, City–Waterloo

A Sketchbook

Leanne Shapton

PENGUIN BOOKS

PENGUIN BOOKS

Published by the Penguin Group
Penguin Books Ltd, 80 Strand, London WC2R ORL, England
Penguin Group (USA) Inc., 375 Hudson Street, New York, New York 10014, USA
Penguin Group (Canada), 90 Eglinton Avenue East, Suite 700, Toronto, Ontario, Canada M4P 2Y3
(a division of Pearson Penguin Canada Inc.)
Penguin Ireland, 25 St Stephen's Green, Dublin 2, Ireland (a division of Penguin Books Ltd)
Penguin Group (Australia), 707 Collins Street, Melbourne, Victoria 3008, Australia
(a division of Pearson Australia Group Pty Ltd)
Penguin Books India Pvt Ltd, 11 Community Centre, Panchsheel Park, New Delhi – 110 017, India
Penguin Group (NZ), 67 Apollo Drive, Rosedale, Auckland 0632, New Zealand
(a division of Pearson New Zealand Ltd)
Penguin Books (South Africa) (Pty) Ltd, Block D, Rosebank Office Park, 181 Jan Smuts Avenue,
Parktown North, Gauteng 2193, South Africa
Penguin Books Ltd, Registered Offices: 80 Strand, London WC2R ORL, England

www.penguin.com

First published in Penguin Books 2013
001

Set in Baskerville 11.75/15pt
Typeset by Claire Mason
Printed in England by Clays Ltd, St Ives plc

ISBN: 978-1-846-14691-6

www.greenpenguin.co.uk

MIX
Paper from
responsible sources
FSC
www.fsc.org FSC™ C018179

Penguin Books is committed to a sustainable
future for our business, our readers and our
planet. This book is made from Forest
Stewardship Council™ certified paper.

ALWAYS LEARNING   **PEARSON**

OUTGOING

Tasselled red loafers, riding gloves, thick tweed, silk scarf, holding leather bag to chest.

Fedora, lipliner, black Fila trainers, reading Flood *by Stephen Baxter.*

Family of four eating assorted biscuits from tin.

Quilted jacket, hands cupped to window, looking out:

3

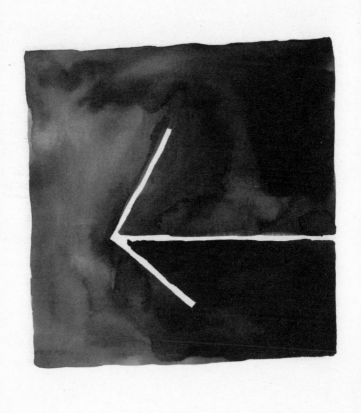

Houndstooth jacket, dyed red hair, Converse All Stars,
earbuds, glancing at other passengers:

No baby. Baby. No baby, no baby, no baby.
Maybe a baby. Too young. Old. Hate fruit.
It's good for you. Always cold. Did I take the
pre-natals. Fucking folic. Usually no children on
this train, what is that family doing here; how
old is the mother, thirty-eight, forty. Allie said
pineapple but is that luteal or follicular. Omega-
3s, kale, berries, there was that piece about
Chinese herbs, herbalist. Hate acupuncture.
Should try it again or maybe some relaxation
exercises or meditation. I'll do it now. Breathe
… Blank white wall … Yellow dress from Cos.
No … How did Sheila get pregnant after those
three IVFs, how did she even afford them,
where do people get their money. Babies and
renovations. Usually at the same time. Sheils
said something about vitamin D. But then Allie
said full-fat dairy and nuts. Ice cream … Blank
white wall … I don't want twins like Allie. One
of them is okay but the other one is a nightmare
and his head is flat at the back. A litter …

Blankness … Do I still have the number for that acupuncturinst. Abu, Abdi. Where's my phone. (Mints, Zyban, E45, reading glasses, lipstick, need to get that one Tom Ford colour Flamingo, keys, floss, stick drive. Phone.)
Hi Danielle, Your FSH level from your last baseline was 8.4. See you next week!
Phonebook. A: Aaron, Abby, Abdi
Will call at lunch. Goji berries, coconut water. No soft cheese. No, that's later. I wonder why Keira isn't pregnant yet. Clomid dose might be too low or something.

Two black computer bags, black jeans, blue shirt unbuttoned to sternum.

Biting nails, reading A Dance with Dragons *by George R.R. Martin.*

Yellow tie, eating a Danish:
So she didn't like the colour. Gotta pick my battles. Can count like seven bad things that have happened since I left Bristol. It's kind of piling up. Harsh of her to be giving me shit

about not responding to emails when she hardly ever responds to mine including the one I sent Monday. Not keeping score, just was hard with all the stress of other stuff. Mary seems cool. Should invite her to the party but have to defer to Jas for the overall arc of the night since last time I made her hang out with my friends and the night ended in tears. Nothing fatal.

I know I should end it. It was weird that time I fucked up my elbow and she didn't even remember, then laughed. And that time she asked me to her work dinner and then there was no space for me at the table, WTF. She's so cute but she's always saying sorry. That ain't right. It's been what almost two years. When I told her I didn't want to talk for a while, after the last fight, she brushed me off. What is that. It's just off. Something's off. Have I ever felt something that is not off though. Maybe in school. Should just focus on my job now. Dad's happy I'm with Lakehead, making OK money, for my age. Lakehead's OK, a stepping stone. Have to get

along with that twat Phil though. God what
a twat. His whole thing is twatty. A few of the
girls think he's hot which is baffling. I suppose he
makes them laugh. Would Jas like him. Christ
what if she would. H. Christ. She didn't even
take me seriously when I told her I didn't want to
talk for a while. Jas, hello, I'm breaking up with
you. Tonight. It'll be nice with Jas, just relax.
I'll meet Mary before and then we'll all grab
a curry or something, get to know each other,
it'll be fine. Maybe they'll be friends, talk about
me. I don't want them to be friends. Jas already
has a thing against Mary and they haven't met.
But I guess it's justified. She senses. She can smell
it, all girls have that sense. What am I going to
do. I think I want out with Jas. I keep saying this
but she changes the subject. That time I told
her I didn't want to talk for a while. How long,
she said. Unsure maybe. Then: can't we talk
about this tomorrow. Dodge a bullet. But she's so
cute when she's all vague. I just gotta end it. No
discussion. She's got on my tits for so long and
she knows it. I gotta be the guy. I'm the one who

gets broken up with usually, the one who gets fired. Maybe it'll feel good being on the other side. She'll cry though, then I'm useless. Her crying. Mary's not like that. Jas knows it's coming.

Ear-clip headset, black square-toed shoes, playing backgammon on iPhone.

Kombucha drink, moustache, tan suit.

Striped plastic carrier bag, pink wedges, smirking.

Lavender shirt, red folder, enormous watch.

Clean shave, FT, Cartier, reading BlackBerry:
From: Ngu, Trang
RE: file
To: Jenkins, Geoffrey
Hi Geoff, For some reason I cannot open the file, but if you are out of town for the next month, we won't be able to work out a meeting anyways, but the idea sounds great. We won't need stats until 6 Sept. You could keep a record and we can do a forward projection. Let me know. Thanks! Best, Trang

Trang. Trang. Black turtleneck. The little
one with the shiny hair. Cute. Looks like the
bartender at Eight. Quiet. Maybe doesn't have
a boyfriend. Looks like the porn girl. So hot.
6 Sept. Set up a meeting. Hot.

From: Jones, Helen
RE: lunch menu
To: Shore, David; McCarey, Colin; Duenwald,
Mike; Hadin, Toby; Lombardo, Mark; Jenkins,
Geoffrey; Wills, Ida; Hodgerakis, George;
Griffiths, Peter
Hi Guys here's the menu, http://kiranindian.
co.uk/
Let me know what you'd like. Helen
Why are Mark and Toby before me on the
list. Helen likes them more, are they nicer
to her. I never noticed Helen, fat bird, retro
glasses, weird type. Does she have any sway
with David. She must, god I've been so dim.
OK. Helen, cute top. Helen, what are you
reading. Seen any good movies, Helen. That
one's not bad. Maybe she's cool. What is with

the dresses she wears like from the fifties, *Mad Men* or whatever, looks like she's got up for Halloween half the time. Sometimes though those weird birds are kinky, with the Madonna underwear or corsets and whatnot. Maybe Helen likes a bit of play, bit of hanky. She's got that arse at least. Maybe some pony business, where's she from. Leeds maybe.

From: Lombardi, Mark
RE: Lucy's last day
To: Crittenden, Lucy Cc: Shore, David; McCarey, Colin; Duenwald, Mike; Jenkins, Geoffrey; Hadin, Toby; Lombardo, Mark; Wills, Ida; Hodgerakis, George; Griffiths, Peter; Patrick, Ian; Jones, Helen; Charlotte, Standing; Moffat, Casey; Edemariam, Heidi; Tibor, Bjorn; Lukas, Attila; Peet, Catherine
Friday, sadly, is Lucy's last day here at Kingfisher. That evening, after close, please join us in mourning our loss – and in buying her more drinks than she has any real intention of consuming.

Where is the easy part: the bar of the Slug. Among the maze of rooms, the bar is the one without tables and with fewer tellys.

When is trickier: Friday closes being what they are, we'll head down there some time between 7 p.m. and 10. Expect a more exact departure time as the date approaches.

Lucy. Which one is Lucy.

Two leather handbags, reading glasses on head, holding teacher's union memo.

Holding coffee cup and banana peel.

Quilted jacket, pointy black shoes, large watch, earbuds: I have not cultivated my talents. I have not tried hard enough. I like Adele's voice because it reminds me of Aunt Harriet, I like sewing because it reminds me of my mum. I am not good at my job. There will be no soap in the soap dispenser again. *The scars of your love remind me of us / They keep me thinking that we almost had it all.* Will go see Gary and Tanisha and the baby after work and bring food. Crisps, more

milk, bread and bananas, bottle of red. Maybe
I can go in my lunch hour. Crisps, more milk,
bread and bananas, bottle of red. Should I buy
the shoes. I bought the blue ones a while ago.
On eBay they were new in the box for £165.
I think it's outrageous the lady wants £250
when she probably got them at a sample sale
for £100. But I love the blue ones – cornflower
or royal – so much I want the green ones too.
They weirdly go with everything and are instant
updaters, which is what I need to get by in
a corporate environment. The blue go with the
yellow dress, the grey suit. Green won't go with
the yellow, but they'll go with the pink. Blue go
with the black but not the brown, green will go
with brown, they'll go with everything, I need to
get them.

*The scars of your love remind me of us/ They keep
me thinking that we almost had it all.* I love Adele.
*The scars of your love remind me of us/ They keep me
thinking that we almost had it all.* Who gives a sofa
to someone anyway, we were totally crazy to
even do that, especially when Tanisha moaned

for weeks about being pregnant and having
to arrange to get it picked up. After moaning
for years about not being pregnant. We never
should have given it. Who gives someone a sofa.
And what is with the emailing and asking if we
want to have dinner when you leave it up to us
to decide on date, restaurant and time. That is
a crap invitation. Crap. Crap invitation.

Two-piece suit, sandals with socks.

Heavy-framed glasses, windswept hair.

Grey shirt, grey suit, grey shoes, listening to MP3.

*Straight long shiny hair, large Yonex tennis bag, reading
texts:*
Please don't silent treatment. I told you the
things I did out of sadness, not anger.
Sent 07:35
I can't stand it any more. If you can't control
your outbursts I'm out. You leave me no room
to respond, all I hear is you coming at me.
Received 08:01
I gave you room, you just defended yourself.

Like always. Sent 08:01

I was explaining my position. Received 08:02

Which is defense, not apology. Sent 08:03

Why can't you just apologize? Sent 08:10

When you are flying off the handle
I can't apologize. Received 08:24

Why can't you apologize before I lose my
temper? Sent 08:25

*Brown shoes, khakis, Prince of Wales check jacket, blue
rubber bracelet.*

Grey dress, large breasts, chunky necklace, crying.

Leopard-print scarf, doing Metro *crossword.*

*Black jacket, black trousers, black shoes, blue shirt,
shaved head, holding stopwatch:*

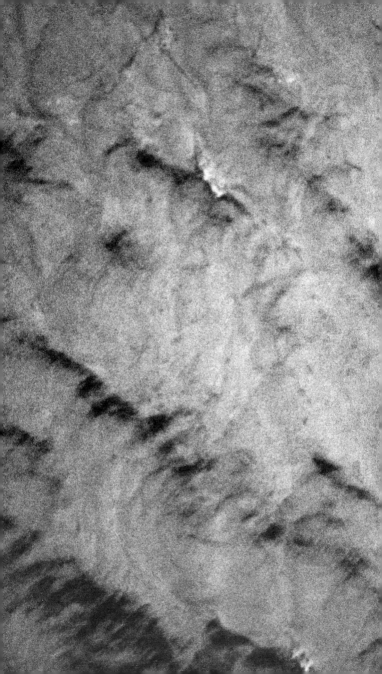

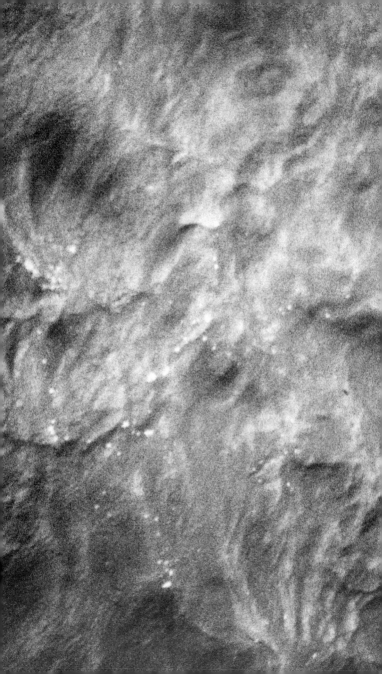

00:03:58. For 2.4 km. I can swim that, I can swim that in 40:00:00. Today at the Grange Club. Hope that wanker isn't there too. If I can go a 23:00:00 for the 1500m I can do 40:00:00 for 2500m. Training is paying off. I can do this.

Yellow-and-black skull cap, shirtsleeves rolled up.

String of pearls, lipstick on teeth.

Glossy head of hair, blue cotton suit, nose in air.

Swiss army backpack, discreetly inserts mint in mouth: Float like a butterfly, sting like a bee. OK. Today: glide through the lobby, affable smile to security. Nod to Tony. All systems normal. Play it cool. That girl looks like Gillian. Wearing that lacy top she had on last Tuesday. Top Shop or Bond Street. Nice. Pink nipples or brown. Pink. Does she like me. Maybe just a bit. Give her boyish grin. That is not Gillian. Eyes down, look away from the tits. Or maybe Dan's in the lift. Dick in a suit. Not even a sharp one. Clothes make the dick. Does he know I'll outmanoeuvre him today, tomorrow and every

day he puts his dickishness in my face. Wonder
if he thinks I like him. I'll ask him out for lunch.
Two Rieslings, lean into him, look into his eyes.
'Hey Dan, are we friends, you and me?' Him,
taken aback. What can he say. 'Course, dude.
You're the coolest guy in the office.' Maybe he
would. Shit. Abort.

Out the lift and into reception. Morning
Jake. Morning Gavin. What does that guy
do all fucking day. Watch porn. Maybe
there's a category for that: drilling the gay
receptionist – law, banking and multinational
editions. Slide down the corridor, polite hellos
to all who dare come before me. The fire inside
is not a fire you see. Into the office, flick the
blinds up. Sun's going to be in your face, pal.
Ten to ten, cowboy time. Settle the nerves.
This is how it will go: Drew comes in, gesture
him to sit down across from me. Got three
inches height on you buddy. Keep up with the
smiles. Don't let him know what I know. Then
out it comes, sotto voce: 'So, Drew, a little
birdie tells me there may be some differences

of opinion with me re: you … Better to hear
it from the horse's mouth than through the
grapevine, yes?' Better to get it straight from the
horse's arse, you shit-talking prick. See it now:
Drew shifting in the chair. Me playing cool,
eyebrow raised. Drew squirming, eyes blinking
against the sun, thinking up lame response.
Give him a minute before I put the knife in …
What's he gonna say. 'Oh Gavin, I think you're
great. There's never been a problem between
us.' Shit, what if he does. Rewind. Gotta go
in harder, faster. No margin for error. Can the
pleasantries. Minute he walks in, I give him the
old samurai stare. Samur-eye. When I look at
you like that, you've been looked at. Don't even
offer him the chair. Straight in: 'Drew, I'm tried
of hearing second-hand the shit you've been
talking about me behind my back … No,
please don't interrupt. I'm talking … This is
how it's going to be.' Drew panicky, like some
fat old prizefighter who knows he's gonna get
knocked down. 'So here's the deal: I have eyes
and ears in every office on this fucking floor.

35

I have this place covered. You wanna start
something, you better be ready to finish. 'Cause
I'm already in the tenth round, and I wasted
guys younger, smarter, tougher than you, and
I got off on doing it. You got that?' Bank. Stay
cool. Samurai. samurai.

White ballet flats, keeps falling asleep.

Fur-lined coat, tote bag, counting on one hand.

Two identical black handbags, runny nose.

Knitted hat, wingtips, toothpaste at corner of mouth.

Black hijab, both black-gloved hands holding pole.

Enormous scarf, two handbags, reading Kindle.

*Large backpack, pink hoody, holding map of London,
reading iPhone:*
You'll like the Waterloo–City line. The majority
of passengers on the W–C line are traveling
between all points converging on Waterloo
Station, and Bank, in the City. The majority of
passengers are on their way to and from work.

This work is usually in the finance sector. There are few children, strollers and elderly. The trip is brief, the occurrences of one-unders are minimal, chatter is rare and the view is nil. The line has a nickname: The Drain. This might refer to the physical properties of the line, running as it does beneath the River Thames in a sort of curve reminiscent of plumbing. Also to the complete emptying out of the cars at both ends. It's like what we have in NY – the S train between Grand Central and Times Square.

Some stats I found for you: Construction on the line began in 1894, when men bore through the clay beneath the Thames at a rate of 10 feet every 24 hours. The line is one of the oldest in the city, but was not part of the London Underground until 1994. Before then it was operated by British Rail.

When you get out walk southwest and head toward Waterloo Bridge; you can cross here to get to the Globe theater and my favorite pub is there too.

If all your favorite things are here why
didn't you come with me. The invitation was
open, you could have said yes instead of being
all like, Oh you're going to have a great time,
I'll make a list of all my favourite places and
things to do and it'll be like I'm there with you.
Not even getting the hint that I was inviting
you to come. You've been here so much when
I told you I wanted to go it was like I was
saying let's go. It was like saying I want you to
come with me. Then we could have got this off
the ground and not had it be such a secret any
more. You could have told your wife it was for
my work, for the guideblog I was working on
and needed a friend to travel with. She's cool,
she would have understood, then we would
have been here together. Then we would have
been on this fucking train together and doing
all of the things you told me about. You know
London so well it's like you've written the
blog already. Shit. You know everything about
London already. You would have been perfect.

Pink tie, pimp roll.

Two handbags, sweat beading on forehead.

Woman with eyes closed, copy of Easy Living *in lap.*

Fat man, both hands twisted outwards resting on knees.
Chewing pen, Asda bag, mole like a tear.

Black wheelie-bag, black boots, pink rose in hair.

Counting passengers, chewing gum:

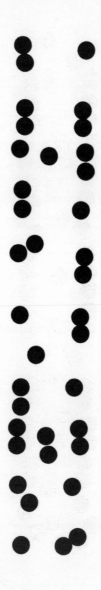

Thirty-seven today.

Sixty-two yesterday.

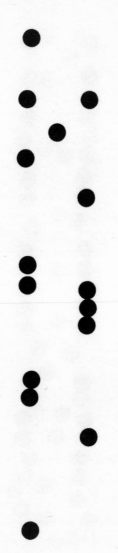

Fifteen Friday.

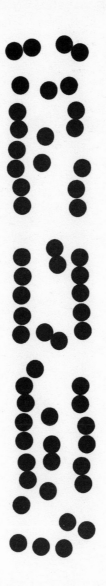

Fifty-seven Thursday.

Three Wednesday.

Hoop earrings, very long nails, reading magazine:
A great neutral sandal. Rock a tropical print.
Rihanna without make-up. Bikini top £3.99. Are
you over ombré? Kate snapped up the Mulberry
satchel. It's all about intense hits of bright colour.
Think tomato red, acid yellow, fluoro pink, cobalt
blue and Quality Street purple. It's a colour
explosion. Love Love Love! Rooney has carved
out a chic signature style. Copy her look.
What's not to love about the new pretty vibe?
A peachy Prada bag. Spa-factor. Luxe metallica is
one trend that always hits the spot. Sleek, stylish
ponies. Louise is a natural blonde. Is there ever
an excuse for cheating? The perfect girls' night
out. Ali McGraw meets Faye Dunaway. One
word: Mexicana. Get it before it goes. There
isn't a stylish woman who's ever been let down by
a crisp white shirt. Bored of cornflakes?
When was the last time I ate cornflakes.
Ben's mum's house that first weekend visit. She
did not like me. I wonder if she'd like me better
after getting the promotion. Didn't think I were
good enough for her baby boy. The way I'd ask

her a question and she'd answer to him. Turn
her body away from me at the table. Then, how
did I like being Ben's secretary. A secretary.
That she was a secretary once too. Should have
kept getting up to answer my BlackBerry the
way Ben did. Maybe get more respect that way.

Beyoncé loves her. I can't afford to split up with
my boyfriend. Luck is an attitude. Wish lists at
the ready … Be seen in skirt £14. Totally tropical
vintage trophy trousers. Ricki keeps things simple
and oh-so chic in this head-to-toe black ensemble.
Super-elegant, waist-nipping and tummy-hiding
… Her High-Street Highness. Where should
Kate's style go from here?

Brown jacket, brown shoes, brown corduroy, lips moving.

Perfect complexion, fingernails bitten to quick.

Purple trench coat, engagagement ring, trainers.

Purple crocodile handbag, eating chocolate eclair.

High-heeled booties, two handbags, red lips:
Just SO didn't game it with Curtis. It's not

me. I can't strategize after a certain point of attachment. Silly fool. It's my cynicism and non corporate-ness and maybe this has nothing to do with that, but Curtis is driving me fucking nuts and I haven't even started working on the team. His whole attitude … so egotistical and proprietary. Rather than acting supportive and caring like let me help nurture your vision he's shooting down things I say, even in casual email or conversation, and then getting all competitive and judgemental if I voice a disagreement with him like when he proposed that currency play I thought was insane. Didn't respond then dropped it entirely.

Maybe I should call him on the phone and talk about our working relationship. Because the idea of him being this 'voice' of NatWest is so annoying and unrelatable to me. And this sense that it is 'his' department, 'his' project and I'm brought on to be his conduit. I am overreacting. His bossiness, combined with Dianne's fearfulness, is starting to feel like a really hard combination for me, with my self-doubt and cynicism, hard to manage. Curtis isn't the director. He's sort of an overseer who helps when there is a restructuring. I think part of the problem for him, which I want to be sympathetic to, is that he is in a position of power with nothing specifically to do. I don't think the others particularly like some higher person coming in and giving helpful advice that they don't know if they have to take or not. I could be wrong, but that's my read. If he were the director that would almost be better, because we could go to it and have a real clash if we needed to. And he would have tons of real stuff to do.

God, I hope I don't see that puffy-lipped slag again. Cheryl, or Sheri. She really thinks it's her duty to be snooty. Michelle betrayal continues unabated and is baffling. I think I may not like her any more. Please let this shift. At least these boots make me look tall.

Pigeon-toed stance, rooster chest.

Shrugging, holding plastic water bottle.

Biting nails, watery eyes.

False eyelashes, knee-high boots, combing hair with fingers:
I should have asked if I could bring Alex. They
probably started talking about me after I left
all like, did she ask you if she could bring Alex
and shrugging and laughing. But didn't Jessa
bring Lexy to the last one at my house and
I don't think she asked me she just included
her in the email chain. It didn't help that
nobody talked to Alex. She looks cold but she
isn't. I should write a thank you note, the nice
paper. Kelly must think I'm an idiot after that
conversation and how I kept saying the word
'poo'. Why did I say it so many times, I had
only had one White Russian. She probably went
home and told Oliver what a weirdo I am and
that she doesn't want to be on my team. That
girl's boots are nice, should I ask her where she
got them, maybe I can take a picture of them
without her noticing. Or I could just ask her.
But what if she's mean or doesn't speak English

then everyone will look at me. My hair. When
Kat asked what is the situation with my hair.
And then that woman in Boots said what's up
with your hair. The woman in the queue in
front of me at Starbucks had the hair I want.
I should have asked her. Or taken a picture.

Scowling, arms folded, overstuffed backpack between feet.

Large pearls, studded suede ballet flats, faded lipstick.

Navy suit, white shirt, no tie, perspiring.

Blue tent dress, large breasts, scrolling iPhone:

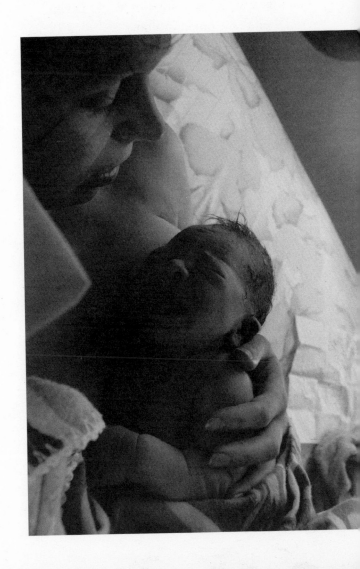

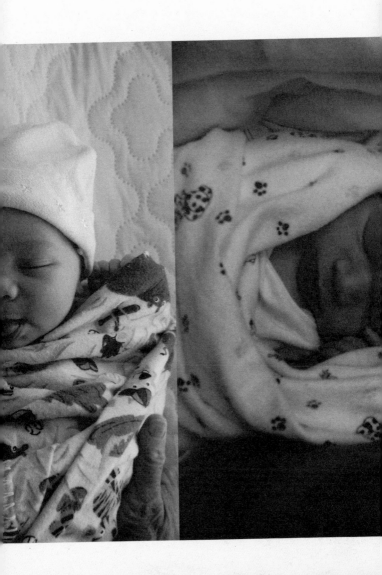

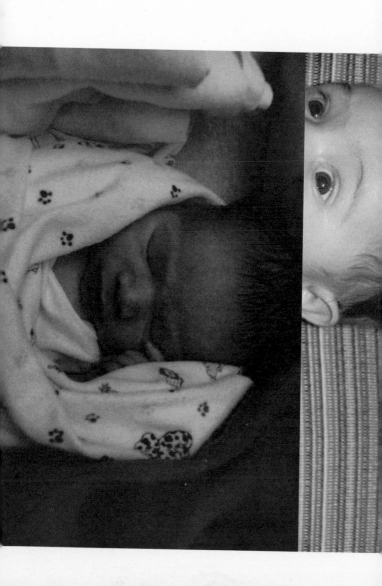

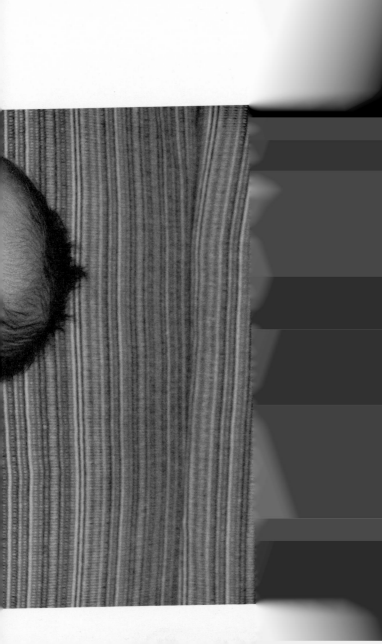

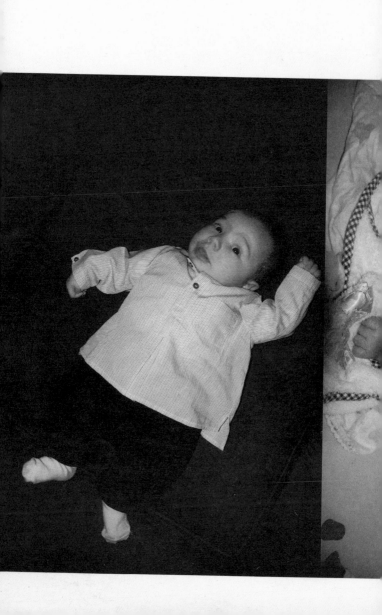

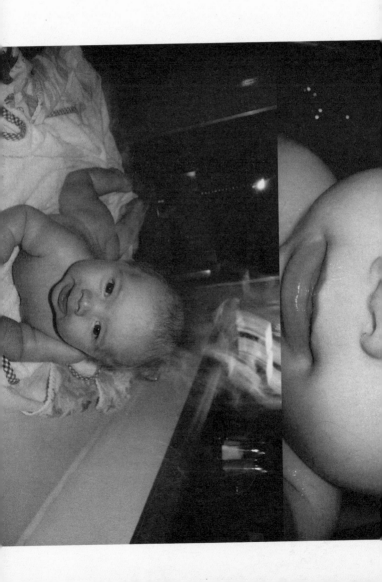

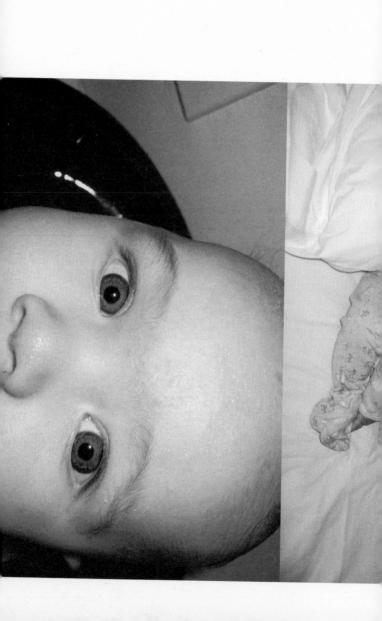

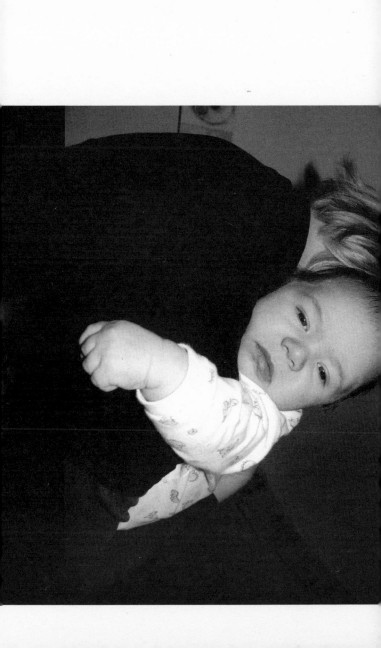

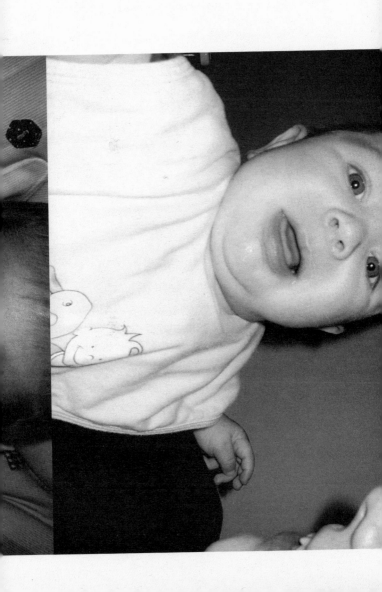

Fleur-de-lys tie, direct eye contact, Zara Home bag.

Black trousers, carrying cup of carrots and celery.

Black pencil skirt, grey scrunchie, reading a copy of
Mrs Dalloway:

> … and his eyes (as eyes tend to be), eyes merely;
> hazel, large; so that he was, on the whole,
> a border case, neither one thing nor the other,
> might end with a house at Purley and a motor
> car, or continue renting apartments in back
> streets all his life; one of those half-educated, self-
> educated men whose education is all learnt from
> books borrowed from public libraries, read in the
> evening after the day's work, on the advice of
> well-known authors consulted by letter.
>
> As for other experiences, the solitary ones,
> which people go through alone, in their bedrooms,
> in their offices, walking the fields and streets of
> London, he had them; had left home, a mere
> boy, because of his mother; she lied; because he
> came down to tea for the fiftieth time with his
> hands unwashed; because he could see no future
> for a poet in Stroud; and so, making a confidant

of his little sister, had gone to London leaving an absurd note behind him, such as great men have written, and the world has read later when the story of their struggles has become famous.

London has swallowed up many millions of young men called Smith; thought nothing of fantastic Christian names like Septimus with which their parents have thought to distinguish them. Lodging off the Euston Road, there were experiences, again experiences, such as change a face in two years from a pink innocent oval to a face lean, contracted, hostile. But of all this what could the most observant of friends have said except what a gardener says when he opens the conservatory door in the morning and finds a new blossom on his plant: It has flowered; flowered from vanity, ambition, idealism, passion, loneliness, courage, laziness, the usual seeds, which all muddled up (in a room off the Euston Road), made him shy, and stammering, made him anxious to improve himself, made him fall in love with Miss Isabel Pole, lecturing in the Waterloo Road upon Shakespeare.

Penny loafers, left penny missing, doodling on a copy of
The Times:

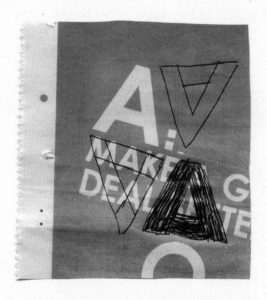

...summer — two strikers, a wing and ... one centre back — to ... for the top four next seaso ... ...my was expected to be the ... ...wards, although the Marsei ... ...alued at about £20 million, s ... last ... ks that he want ... to see if Tottenham qualifie ... the Champio ... League before he d... on his futur... Tottenham also h... ...bs about t... player's heart def... ...most led his transfer fro... ...lles falling through...

Tottenham ... old fresh talks in Holland today to sign Jan Vertonghen afte... ...efender, who will ente... ...his deal at Ajax th... summ... ...preferred destin...

Redk... ...ttenham finishing ... ...x two of the past three seasons — because they did not have the distraction of Europe after Christmas. Next season, he is likely to ...t his strategy of picking a

...ric is attracting ...tion from big clubs ...and could be

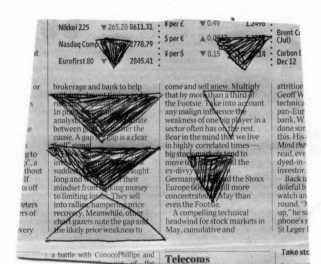

		¥ per £	▼ 0.49	1.2496	
Nikkei 225	▼ 265.28 8611.31	$ per €	▲ 0.0922		Brent C
Nasdaq Comp	2778.79				(Jul)
Eurofirst 80 ▼	2845.41	¥ per $	▼ 0.15	14	Carbon E Dec 12

or
s

e

g to
p", a
thout

ts off

reters
rs of

every

brokerage and bank to help
ri

In pri
analyst
between g
cause. A gap
"sell" signal

in
sudden
long and w
mindset from
to limiting lo
into rallies, hampering price
recovery. Meanwhile, other
chart gazers note the gap and
the likely price weakness to

come and sell anew. Multiply
that by more than a third of
the Footsie. Take into account
any malign influence the
weakness of one big player in a
sector often has on the rest.
Bear in the mind that we live
in highly correlated times —
big stock markets tend to
move to
ex-divvy
Germany
Europe 600
concentrated
even the Footsie.

A compelling technical
headwind for stock markets in
May, cumulative and

and the Stoxx
till more
May than

attrition

Geoff W
technica
pan-Eur
bank, W
done son
this. His
Mind the
read, eve
dyed-in-
investor.

Back i
doleful b
watch an
round. "
up," he sa
phone's r
St Leger

a battle with ConocoPhillips and

Telecoms

Take st

For up-to

e Secrets

FTSE 100
Close 5,267.62

Dow Jones
Midday 12,422.36

Eurofirst 80
Close 2,845.41

Nikkei
Close 8,611.31

▪ he dumpot pub has
st..d in the City
sin..... ..A the
se...... ..ot of
br..... ..the
w may ....een there
as lo.. ..14 years in
..rket I ..ve never seen it
s," one complains,
a long pull on another
.p. "It's desperate. It's
..ell in bloody May . . ."
nodding to the stock
's most trite, yet
ly apposite, adage. Sell
an..go away, don't
ack until St Leger Day.
un..daft but,
..cally speaking, studies
hat the market does
between May and the
..g of the last classic of
..se racing flat season ..
..ber. Historically, most
..make their dough in
..three months. Money
..o shares before the end
..ix year in April and

The week's biggest movers

Company

Cha

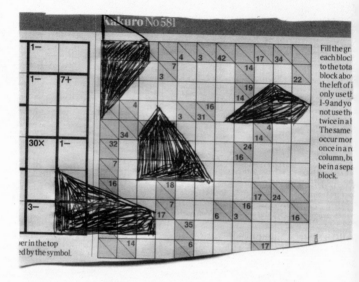

Ethnic-print dress, red umbrella, snow-white hair.

Wet hair, wet feet, freckles.

Wooden-bead necklace, t-shirt, two-piece suit.

Hands pressed together, briefcase across knees, squinting.

Large front teeth, mouth breathing.

**PENGUIN
LINES**

Leanne
Shapton

AGE:	39
HEIGHT:	5 foot 8 inches
EYE COLOUR:	Brown
FIRST VISIT TO THE CITY:	August 1988
LENGTH OF TIME LIVED IN LONDON:	2 years
FAVOURITE MODE OF TRANSPORT:	Double-decker bus
SELF-RATED TUBE GEEKINESS:	2 out of 10
DAY JOB:	Illustrator
COVER CHOSEN BY:	Me
IDEA FOR BOOK:	The endless toggle between two stations
FIRST LINE IN THE BOOK:	'Tassled red loafers, riding gloves, thick tweed, silk scarf, holding leather bag to chest.'

Front cover:
Leanne Shapton
Cover design:
Jim Stoddart
Author photo:
Jochen Braun

**PENGUIN
LINES**

Leanne
Shapton

AGE:	39
HEIGHT:	5 foot 8 inches
EYE COLOUR:	Brown
FIRST VISIT TO THE CITY:	August 1988
LENGTH OF TIME LIVED IN LONDON:	2 years
FAVOURITE MODE OF TRANSPORT:	Double-decker bus
SELF-RATED TUBE GEEKINESS:	2 out of 10
DAY JOB:	Illustrator
COVER CHOSEN BY:	Me
IDEA FOR BOOK:	The endless toggle between two stations
FIRST LINE IN THE BOOK:	'Bifocals, reading article on how to cure chronic back pain.'

Front cover:
Leanne Shapton
Cover design:
Jim Stoddart
Author photo:
Jochen Braun

150 UNDERGROUND

The Blue Riband
by Peter York
(the Piccadilly line)

*What We Talk About When
We Talk About The Tube*
by John Lanchester
(the District line)

*A Good Parcel of
English Soil*
by Richard Mabey
(the Metropolitan line)

**Tube
Knowledge**

**A Breath of
Fresh Air**

*A Good Parcel of
English Soil*
by Richard Mabey
(the Metropolitan line)

**Design for
Life**

Waterloo–City, City–Waterloo
by Leanne Shapton
(the Waterloo & City line)

Buttoned-Up
by Fantastic Man
(the East London line)

Drift
by Philippe Parreno
(the Hammersmith & City line)

*A History of Capitalism
According to the Jubilee Line*
by John O'Farrell
(the Jubilee line)

A Northern Line Minute
by William Leith
(the Northern line)

Mind the Child
by Camila Batmanghelidjh and
Kids Company
(the Victoria line)

Heads and Straights
by Lucy Wadham
(the Circle line)

**Laughter and
Tears**

**Breaking
Boundaries**

Drift
by Philippe Parreno
(the Hammersmith & City line)

Buttoned-Up
by Fantastic Man
(the East London line)

Waterloo–City, City–Waterloo
by Leanne Shapton
(the Waterloo & City line)

Earthbound
by Paul Morley
(the Bakerloo line)

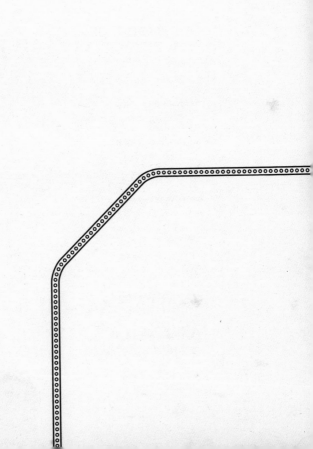

Waterloo–City, City–Waterloo

A Sketchbook

Leanne Shapton

PENGUIN BOOKS

PENGUIN BOOKS

Published by the Penguin Group
Penguin Books Ltd, 80 Strand, London WC2R 0RL, England
Penguin Group (USA) Inc., 375 Hudson Street, New York, New York 10014, USA
Penguin Group (Canada), 90 Eglinton Avenue East, Suite 700, Toronto, Ontario, Canada M4P 2Y3
(a division of Pearson Penguin Canada Inc.)
Penguin Ireland, 25 St Stephen's Green, Dublin 2, Ireland (a division of Penguin Books Ltd)
Penguin Group (Australia), 707 Collins Street, Melbourne, Victoria 3008, Australia
(a division of Pearson Australia Group Pty Ltd)
Penguin Books India Pvt Ltd, 11 Community Centre, Panchsheel Park, New Delhi – 110 017, India
Penguin Group (NZ), 67 Apollo Drive, Rosedale, Auckland 0632, New Zealand
(a division of Pearson New Zealand Ltd)
Penguin Books (South Africa) (Pty) Ltd, Block D, Rosebank Office Park, 181 Jan Smuts Avenue,
Parktown North, Gauteng 2193, South Africa

Penguin Books Ltd, Registered Offices: 80 Strand, London WC2R 0RL, England

www.penguin.com

First published in Penguin Books 2013
001

Copyright © Leanne Shapton, 2013

The moral right of the author has been asserted

Set in Baskerville 11.75/15pt
Typeset by Claire Mason
Printed in England by Clays Ltd, St Ives plc

ISBN: 978–1–846–14691–6

www.greenpenguin.co.uk

Penguin Books is committed to a sustainable
future for our business, our readers and our
planet. This book is made from Forest
Stewardship Council™ certified paper.

MIX
Paper from
responsible sources
FSC
www.fsc.org
FSC® C018179

ALWAYS LEARNING

PEARSON

RETURN

Bifocals, reading article on how to cure chronic back pain.

Black suit, rotating index finger inside ear, then subtly sniffing finger.

Navy blue dress, distracted expression, black bra-strap showing.

Quilted jacket folded in lap, hands cupped to window, looking out:

3

*Red lipstick, staring hard at nude-stockinged ankles and
Nike trainers.*

Fingers laced, chewing gum.

Navy suit, striped tie, scrolling BlackBerry.

*Houndstooth jacket, dyed red hair, Converse All Stars,
earbuds, glancing at other passengers:*
Too young, too young, too young. Baby. Baby.
Probably all grown. Acupuncture next Monday,
ultrasound Thursday afternoon. Cancel
meeting with Bob. Does Bob have kids, maybe
he'll understand if I tell him but no I'll just say
doctor's appointment. Not even telling Mum.
Karen looks pregnant, she might just be first
tri, not telling anyone, but looks a little green
around the gills wearing a scarf in front of her
belly, I could just ask her but that's not done,
not done. I wish I could tell someone, only
Rach knows and she's away. Dying to ask Bella
if she flew when she was in her first tri. And
what she did for nausea. Not puking at least, but
the nausea my god, wish it were dead of winter

so I could wear my sea-bands without anyone noticing. The nausea out of control. I'm going to pack on the pounds if I keep eating bagels but bagels is all that settles my tum. Heartbeat last week. Dennis wasn't there, wish he were there. He did look sad when I told him, but still. Weird I want him so near now this is happening when I just wanted his sperm and to get away from him before. Animal thing. Is it pineapple I'm supposed to eat or just the middle of pineapple. Or is it eggs. Read somewhere about a woman eating six egg yolks a day. Jesus H. If I tell Rick in five weeks, that puts us into the negotiations with Templeton. Shit. Not going to go well. Rick has kids though, right, Rick has kids. And three nannies. And a wife who doesn't work. There was that picture of her in *Tatler*. Jesus H. Fancy dress, looking a mess. Nobody looks good in fancy dress. Not even her. Rach told me she was afraid Ken would leave her at eight months when she was fat. He didn't though. How fat am I going to get. I already feel so bloated and burpy. This part

is not fun. I need a bikky. Four fucking bikkies.
Cauliflower cheese for supper I think.

Sunglasses on head, collar popped.

Black trench, arms crossed over chest, knees
hyperextended.

Perfect ponytail, perfect posture, pink flats.

Pale blue shirt, reading A Dance with Dragons *by*
George R.R. Martin.

Yellow tie, biting fingernails:
Told her I don't want to talk for a while. How
long, she said. Unsure maybe. Then, can't we
talk about this tomorrow. I have a headache
and I'm exhausted. Of course. Jas. I don't know
how long, for at least a couple of weeks, or
until you feel like you can bring something
to the conversation. You hurt me so much,
been so careless. I've given you the benefit of
the doubt. Am trying to leave this smoothly,
give you a chance to not feel railroaded. But
this isn't helping. You've just hurt me more,

being more defensive. Selfish. Gotta get my stuff out of there, leave the key. I know I can be a real sucker. Trying to live less by the hour more by the day but the hour looks pretty good sometimes. Mary, the poetry professor at Birkbeck. Dated Kev four years ago. Trying to get out of that relationship for a while. Made out after we got drunk with Neil's band. Then the party and slow dance and made out in front of folks, embarrassing. She's smart. Fit. Not sure what I'm ready for. Well I told her, I said, well you know how I feel. And I think she got that, and she said the same. Her in her puffy jacket with the fur around the head so cute. This guy is such a bore and bad to her. I fancy her. She should go steady with me but if she wants to stay in it for some reason then let it be innit. Valentine's Day is coming up. The card Jas gave me with a Christmas gift, something like I promise no more taking for granted-ness, no more crankiness next year. Send Jas an email telling her not to get in touch any more. Erase her from phone, text, instant message and put

all the stuff she gave me away. I didn't say leave me alone I said leave me be.

Dinner tonight with Dev. He'll have some good advice. Look at him and Cheryl. What's it been two years; they seem cool. A cat even. But do I want that. Yeah I want that. Didn't want that when Louise wanted that but maybe want it now. Louise was pushy. Tried to make it perfect. Weird seeing her in Tesco, buying a cake and celery. Still cute but not in the same way, what was it maybe jeans, jeans and little shoes when she would always wear heels. Looked older. Lovely to see you she said, when did she start saying lovely.

Sad face, holding lilies.

Green terry-cloth scrunchie, black briefcase.

Braids wrapped around head, wool scarf tied in bow.

Chewing gum, holding Coke Zero, Cartier, reading BlackBerry:
Hi Geoff, I work in marketing at Kilworth, and

am part of the team that puts together our
subscription programme. My colleague Jill
has been working with LMF on the Loughman
project – but she's out on mat leave and
I'm trying to fill in the gaps so we can make our
deadline. (Which was a couple days ago.) As
I understand it, last week Jill sent the proposal
but Loughman wrote back today with concerns
that we'd strayed too far from your original
concept. We were under the impression that
we could alter it as we saw fit – so we made
some changes. We wanted to create an abstract
that bore a strong resemblance to your ideas
for the existing framework, but also change it
enough so that our subscribers felt like they
were getting something exclusive. Charlotte and
Jennifer want to make sure you approve of the
proposal before we present. It can be accessed
via our FTP here:
ftp://ftp.Kilworth.com/graphics/Loughman%20
DO/HOPE%20LAND%20SKYPE%20DO%20
RMX%20FINAL%20%20Folder/
Could you take a look and let us know what

you think? If you disapprove of anything, we'll
need to start from scratch on Monday and turn
out a new version under a tight deadline, so if
you could get back to us as soon as possible,
we'd appreciate it. Please let me know if you
have any questions, problems with the FTP, or
… have no idea what I'm talking about. Thanks,
Megan

Megan. The tall one with Jill that day. Fit.
Holes from eyebrow piercing. What if I ran into
her. If she was on the train now. Where does
she live. Hey, Megan right. Right! I like your
(point to eyebrow shyly). Oh yeah, what do you
like about it. Kissing hard in the gents. Or is
Megan the other one with the green cardigan,
smells like pine tree. Megan. Megan. I think
it's the eyebrow one. Fit. Do you ever wear
the ring in. Sometimes. Oh yeah. What would
I have to do to see you wearing it. I don't know,
first buy me a drink. What'll you have. Whisky.
Would she drink whisky. I don't have any whisky
at home. She probably likes white wine, all
birds like white wine, or, like, Coronas. There

was that one in New York who liked that
Mike's Hard Lemonade. Tasted like candy. She
tasted like candy too but then she threw up then
acted like I didn't notice. She was sad. And they
think the English have the drinking problems.
New York girls are tougher though. Meaner.
I like a little mean, maybe Megan is mean.

No neck, nine zippers on backpack.

Very long brown hair, white jacket, black skirt, tapping foot.

Quilted jacket, pointy black shoes, large watch, earbuds:
Fucking Tanisha. Well, I'm sorry you miss
me, but really can't say that I miss you back.
I'm sorry if that is hurtful to hear but I really
have not missed you for one instant and
I'm glad you had the baby so I could use that as
an excuse to cool the friendship a bit. I'm sorry
if that is hurtful. Do I want to have lunch again.
Honestly. Honestly. No. I don't like you much
any more. I don't like thinking of how one-sided
the friendship was for so long. I don't like being

the friend you always complain to about being
tired, about being fat, about being sad, about
having shingles, about how much your husband
hates his job, and then on top of all that you
thanking me for being so understanding and
forgiving when you sit like a lump and ask me
nothing while your husband drinks my wine,
eats my food and insults me. Fucking Gary. Of
course you miss me. I fucking want the green
ones. Fucking getting them if someone has not
bought them now already.

I don't understand why you're so comfortable
taking and taking and never giving. I'm actually
not very forgiving. Who says to me at the
engagement party 'I'm so tired' like I give a shit.
Who offers to throw a hen party when she has
shingles and is in constant pain, then complains
to friends that her feelings were hurt when
I don't take her up on the offer. What is that
woman wearing. Those boots are criminal.

Head in hands, bag between feet.

Hoop earrings, very long nails, reading magazine:
Scorpio (24 Oct to 22 Nov): Although you'll
do yourself no favours by talking endlessly
about how hard you've worked, you need to
remind certain people that they haven't been
doing their fair share. It's important to do so
in a way that enables you and those concerned
to enjoy yourselves as you get quite a lot done.
A healthy, harmonious atmosphere will make all
the difference. Virgo (24 Aug to 23 Sept): Rather
than struggle with a proposition that's too labour
intensive or costly, consider pooling resources wth
someone you can trust. And be quite blunt about
the fact that you don't want to go ahead single-
handedly and that it could benefit the two of
you if you were to form a working partnership.
Make sure terms and conditions are thrashed
out before you begin. Ever wonder how Victoria
Beckham works a year-round golden glow?
Repairing raspberry. Skin-strengthening ginger.
Wearing a good sports bra is vital, whatever your
size. So cool it hurts. Glow on!

What am I going to wear to Paul's wedding. If
Ben's best man where do I sit. Will his mum
be there, God hope not but possible. Maybe
green, green dress, tan pumps. Something like
what Kate wore in LA, what was that. Or the
blue I bought but never wore. Strapless but
cute, is cute right. No. I don't even want to
marry Ben. Don't even want to marry. His mum
probably wants me to dress like Kate. Boring.
Like the girl in accounts, Phyllida, she's every
man's mum's dream. Skinny too. I wonder if
she is dating. Maybe some older guy, would be
funny though if she was dating an indie rocker.
I'm way more Alexa than Kate. And that's what
Ben likes about me.

*Pink and yellow fingernails, sipping smoothie wrapped in
paper napkin.*

Chin in hand, eyes closed, purple tie.

Striped polo shirt, grey trousers, keeps shrugging.

*Straight long shiny hair, large Yonex tennis bag, reading
texts:*

Pippa's asked us over tonight and I'm afraid
she'll pop the godparent Q. Sent 17:25
They may well ask. Saying no would be tricky.
Received 17:34
She must know something is off. Esp after the
wknd! Sent 17:35
Don't see we have a choice. She is one of your
oldest friends. Received 17:38
I don't think we're in a good place to say yes.
Sent 17:42
Getting tube now. Sent 17:42
Lets talk about this later. Sent: 17:45
Ok, what do you want for supper? Sent 17:46

Leopard-print dress, spotted bag, scrolling BlackBerry.

*Black jacket, black trousers, black shoes, blue shirt,
shaved head, holding stopwatch:*

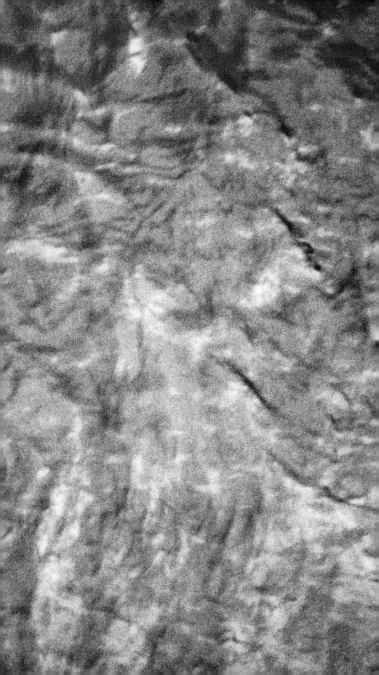

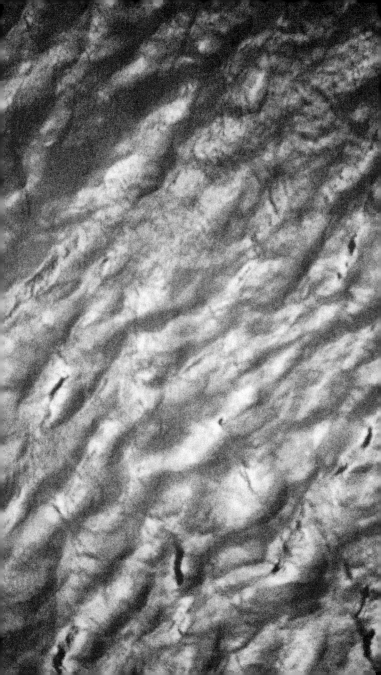

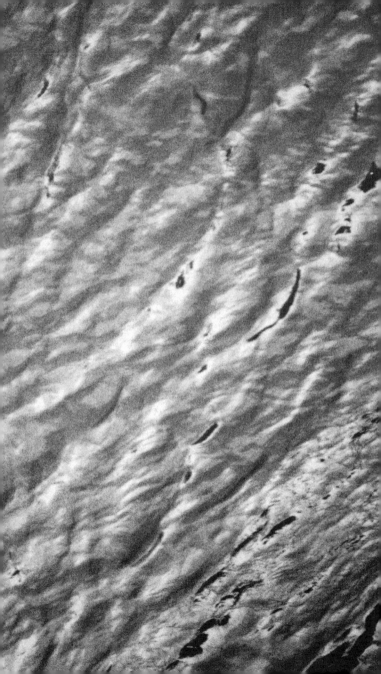

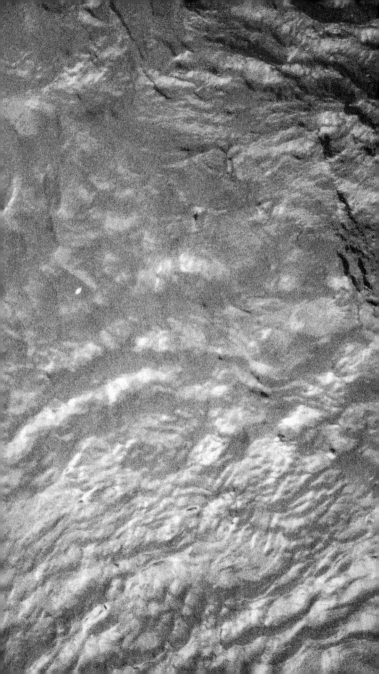

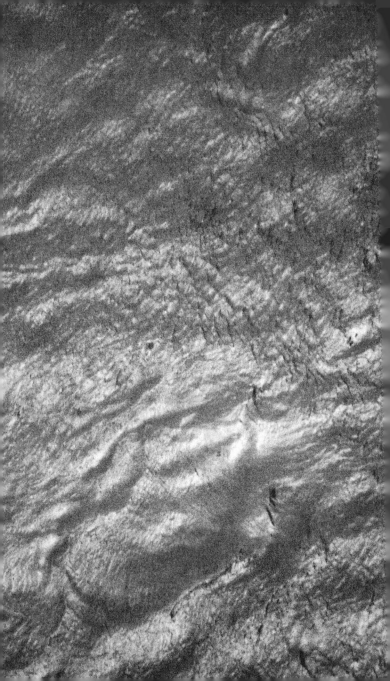

Glasses tucked into V-neck, wedding-band tan line.

Sunglasses atop head, sunglasses on face.

Navy suit, white shirt, no tie, sweating.

00:03:55. Someone will swim that fast one day. But it would mean the 1500m in something like two minutes. Maybe not. Tomorrow get closer to 50:00:00. Take an extra half hour at lunch. If I can do 50:00:00 can certainly do the 1500 in 21:00:00 or 20:00:00. 20:30:00. Beat Tim that fucker.

Purple trench coat, engagement ring, trainers.

One small handbag, one large handbag, glaring at floor.

Pret A Manger paper bag, leggings, golden headphones.

Green-and-blue top, grey-and-black shoes, red-and-brown handbag.

Blue tent dress, large breasts, scrolling iPhone:

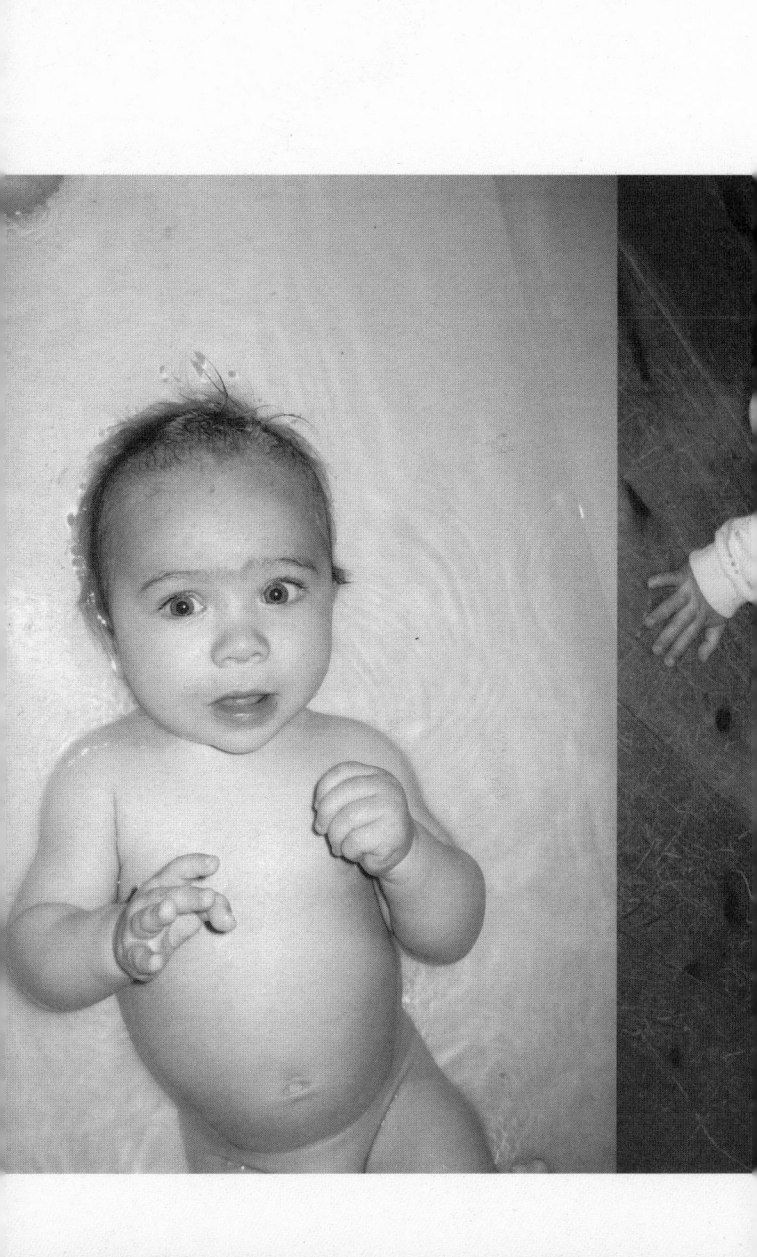

High-heeled booties, two handbags, red lips:
Why did he say that movie wasn't good.
I wanted him to think it was good.
Embarrassing that I told him my mum and
I cried at the end and spontaneously started
hugging. Was he making fun of me. God,
he's so fucking smug. 'Yeah, well it's a small
movie, you can't …' 'Compare it with a good
movie?' 'Yeah, well it's a small movie you
can't …' 'Be moved by it? Put it in the same
league?' Fuck. I just want to keep having that
conversation over and over until he says what
I want. But what do I want him to say. He feels
just like I do and then what. Then we sit there
feeling the same way. Am I going to get to Ikea
this weekend. It's going to suck and I'm not
going to find what I need anyway. Am I going
to be thinking about texting him all weekend.
Dammit. I should just text him now. I'll suggest
we see it again, together. I'll insult his taste in
movies so he'll be a little threatened. But he
already insulted mine.

When we played that game about what bad

movies you like what did he say, *Elf*. And *Music and Lyrics*. But that made me like him. We need to move on to food, we need to get to a restaurant and do something less cerebral. I just want to get him drunk. I already know he likes me I think. But he's senior and it would be bad, still, bad in a fun way. He's not the director. Ikea. I don't want to buy Ikea furniture any more. When does it end. When do I stop buying Ikea furniture for god's sake. I want stuff like in Nathalie's place. Older, heavy stuff. But her husband's rich. Leo's a teacher. Leo. Leo loathes Martin. Of course. Teases me about him. Have to stop flirting. Marriage feels like it's crumbling.

Counting passengers, blowing small chewing gum bubbles:

Fourteen today.

Twenty-five yesterday.

Twenty Friday.

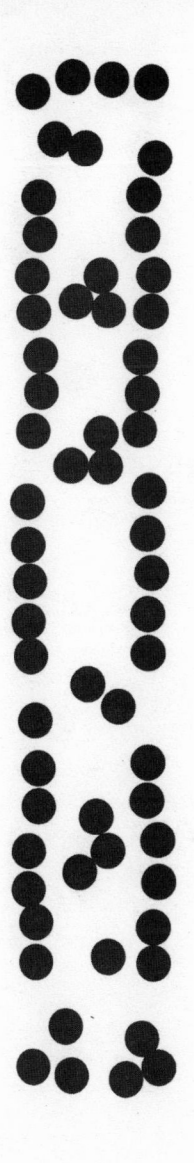

Sixty-two Thursday.

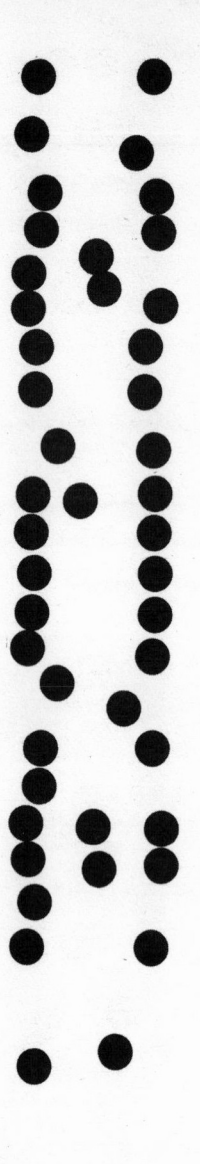

Forty-six Wednesday.

False eyelashes, knee-high boots, texting:
~~Sure, let's have dinner next week.~~
~~Dinner next week sounds fun!~~
~~Yes to dinner next week, I'm there. Name~~
~~a place.~~
~~Longing to have dinner next week.~~
~~Dinner next week 4 sure. Shall we try the new~~
~~Ottolenghi?~~
~~I can only do Weds and Thurs for dinner next~~
~~week.~~
~~Would love to have dinner next week. Thursday?~~
~~Fuck yeah dinner next week! Sounds good. Or~~
~~I can make dinner at mine?~~
~~K!~~
Dinner next week sounds fun!

Curly blonde hair, pale arms, reading opinion section of newspaper.

Knuckles in mouth, legs crossed.

Keys attached to belt, loud voice.

Grey cardigan, soft voice.

Scowling, fingers interlaced, overstuffed backpack between feet.

Swiss army backpack, chewing gum:
You know that your time is coming round / So don't let the bastards grind you down … Cool. *Joshua Tree* or *Achtung Baby* … *Achtung!* Oh, misspent youth. Cried the poet. (Use that in an email to Selena.) Summer of '92 … Corfu. The royal send-off for family holidays. Mummy all bent out of shape. Sorry Mummy. Animal spirits, and all. Elisabeth from Hamburg in a bikini, blonde and bashful. Elisabeth from Hamburg out of her bikini. Bashful always just the first gear. Didn't know that then. Sand and pubes and snogging 'neath the lofty skies. Father makes three. Crazy German on the warpath. Protect the face, protect the balls, hide the boner … The samurai achieves all his goals, while running butt naked for his life. Mum, I really am sorry. *I didn't mean to cause you any sorrow … I didn't mean to cause you any pain.* Elisabeth, Elisabetta, where are you tonight. Wedded to some fat welder in Hamburg,

no doubt. Better him than me. Does Selena
want me to marry her. Do I tell her I'm liable
to get shit-canned tomorrow. *Don't let the bastards
grind you down.* Very helpful, dude. We'll see you
in HR tomorrow. 'Bono, employment at this
company is contingent on meeting rigorous
professional standards of civility, courtesy
and respect. Your conduct today has led us
to question whether you are the right fit for
us going forward.' Bono staring, inscrutable
behind shades. 'And furthermore, ordering
ten thousand pizzas onstage while making
unauthorized use of a company credit card is
an indefensible breach of protocol.' Bono lights
a cigarette and smiles. I could see myself as
a writer. Comedy mostly. TV first, Hollywood
later. Then maybe direct. Aston Martin cruising
down Sunset Boulevard, heading home to the
Hollywood Hills. Hot babe in the seat next to
me, model-actress-brain-surgeon type. Her
name is Charlene. No, Ramona. Whatever.
First Oscar acceptance speech will go: 'Firstly,
I'd like to thank all the losers at Timmerson-

Bodley International, whose small-mindedness
led me to leave behind a sad career in financial
services to make the whole world laugh and cry
and sing. And secondly.' Secondly.

*Black-and-white wrap dress, tapping fingers as though
on a piano.*

Tidy bun, long eyelashes, colour blocking.

Blue shirt, both arms above head holding on to pole.

Black pencil skirt, grey scrunchie, reading a copy of Mrs
Dalloway*:*

> … It has flowered; flowered from vanity,
> ambition, idealism, passion, loneliness, courage,
> laziness, the usual seeds which all muddled up
> (in a room off the Euston Road), made him shy,
> and stammering, made him anxious to improve
> Something was up, Mr Brewer knew; Mr Brewer,
> managing clerk at Sibleys and Arrowsmiths,
> auctioneers, valuers, land and estate agents;
> something was up, he thought, and, being
> paternal with his young men, and thinking very
> highly of Smith's abilities, and prophesying that

he would, in ten or fifteen years, succeed to the
leather armchair in the inner room under the
skylight with the deed-boxes round him, "if he
keeps his health," said Mr Brewer, and that was
the danger – he looked weakly; advised football,
invited him to supper and was seeing his way to
consider recommending a rise of salary, when
something happened which threw out many of
Mr Brewer's calculations, took away his ablest
young fellows, and eventually, so prying and
insidious were the fingers of the European War,
smashed a plaster cast of Ceres, ploughed a hole
in the geranium beds, and utterly ruined the
cook's nerves at Mr Brewer's establishment at
Muswell Hill.

Septimus was one of the first to volunteer
… so prying and insidious were the fingers
of the European War, smashed a plaster cast
of Ceres, ploughed a hole in the geranium
beds, and utterly ruined the cook's nerves at
Mr Brewer's establishment at Muswell Hill
… Septimus was one of the first to volunteer.
He went to France to save an England which

consisted almost entirely of Shakespeare's plays and Miss Isabel Pole in a green dress walking in a square. There in the trenches the change which Mr Brewer desired when he advised football was produced instantly; he developed manliness; he was promoted; he drew the attention, indeed the affection of his officer, Evans by name. It was a case of two dogs playing on a hearth-rug; one worrying a paper screw, snarling, snapping, giving a pinch, now and then, at the old dog's ear; the other lying somnolent, blinking at the fire, raising a paw, turning and growling good-temperedly. They had to be together, share with each other, fight with each other, quarrel with each other. But when Evans (Rezia, who had only seen him once, called him 'a quiet man', a sturdy red-haired man, undemonstrative in the company of women), when Evans was killed, just before the Armistice, in Italy, Septimus, far from showing any emotion or recognizing that here was the end of a friendship, congratulated himself upon feeling very little and very reasonably.

Knees wide apart, picking cuticles.

Penny loafers, left penny missing, doodling on a copy of the Metro:

hell of a banger...

BUTCHER Martin Trendall has certainly put the thing in bangers. He claims to have developed the world's hottest sausages, using four scorching Indian bhut jolokia chillies, paprika and chilli

warned to only eat one per sitting. 'I would challenge anyone to come up with a hotter sausage,' said Mr Trendall, from Oundle, Northamptonshire.

ce to win
omplete this Metroku
the digits that should
ded squares.
be selected
m the correct entries

METROKU
space, the
(reading le
postcode
B DAVID W8 5TT. Texts
rd network charges
Promotional Rules
e details visit www.

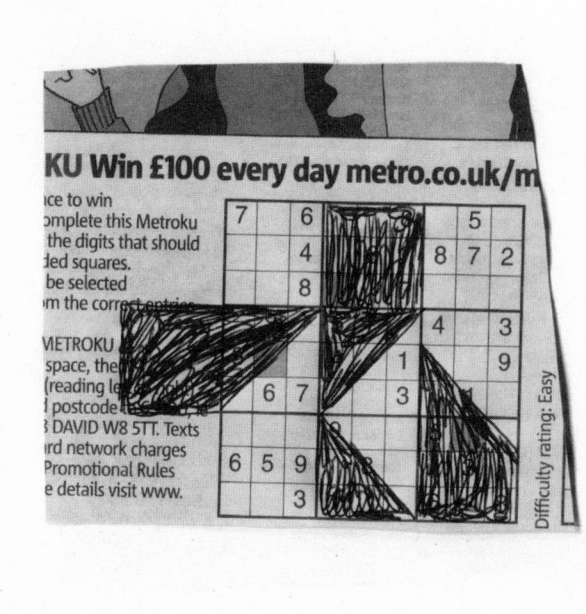

Difficulty rating: Easy

Pressed pink shirt, spotless tote bag, green earplugs.

Blue shirt, pink tie, sunglasses like the front of a car.

Acknowledgements

Many thanks to Jason Logan, Miranda Purves,
Michael Schmelling, Helen Conford, Sarah
Chalfant, Luke Ingram, and James Truman.

PENGUIN LINES

Choose Your Journey

If you're looking for...

Romantic Encounters

Heads and Straights
by Lucy Wadham
(the Circle line)

Waterloo–City, City–Waterloo
by Leanne Shapton
(the Waterloo & City line)

Tales of Growing Up and Moving On

Heads and Straights
by Lucy Wadham
(the Circle line)

A Good Parcel of English Soil
by Richard Mabey
(the Metropolitan line)

Mind the Child
by Camila Batmanghelidjh and
Kids Company
(the Victoria line)

The 32 Stops
by Danny Dorling
(the Central line)